Living in the time of the Pilgrim Fathers

Glenys Ambrus

**Illustrated by
Victor Ambrus**

A & C Black · London

The 'Living in' series by R J Unstead

Living in a Castle	ISBN 0 7136 1088 3
Living in a Crusader Land	ISBN 0 7136 1081 6
Living in a Medieval City	ISBN 0 7136 1090 5
Living in a Medieval Village	ISBN 0 7136 1089 1
Living in Aztec Times	ISBN 0 7136 1426 9
Living in the time of the Pilgrim Fathers	ISBN 0 7136 1427 7

A & C Black Ltd
4, 5 & 6 Soho Square
London W1V 6AD

ISBN 0 7136 1427 7

Printed Offset Litho and bound in Great Britain by Cox & Wyman Ltd, London, Fakenham and Reading

Contents

The Separatist Puritans

During the reign of Elizabeth I everyone was expected to attend the Church of England services regularly; anyone who did not or who held different views of religion could be punished—though the law was not always enforced.

Some churchmen wanted to reform the services of the Church of England. As they hoped to *purify* the Church, they were called *Puritans*. Another group of reformers wanted to *separate* from the Church altogether and to worship as they chose.

In 1603, the Puritans hoped that the new king, James I, would support them in their efforts to reform the Church and to elect ministers from the congregation; this was already the practice in the Presbyterian Church of Scotland to which the king had belonged. But James would not allow the people to elect their own ministers. Such a practice would undermine his own authority. So he ordered that all services were to be in accordance with the Church of England Prayer Book and all private religious meetings banned.

Some Puritan ministers decided to stay in the Church, praying for the opportunity to reform it at a later date. Others felt that there was no alternative but to leave the Church and to *separate*.

One of these was Richard Clyfton, rector of Babworth, a small village in Nottinghamshire. In 1606 he became pastor of a small *Separatist* group at Scrooby, a village in the same county.

William Brewster at Scrooby

William Brewster, postmaster at Scrooby, made arrangements for the services, himself providing refreshments for people who travelled long distances to attend. Clyfton and John Robinson (another former Church of England minister) preached to the group. The three men befriended an orphan named William Bradford of Austerfield, who was to become one of the leaders of the brethren in America.

Persecution and flight

Informers and spies watched the Separatists at Scrooby and even attended their services, until the autumn of 1607 when Brewster was dismissed from his position as postmaster. The group spent many hours in prayer and fasting in order to seek God's guidance; eventually they decided to escape to Holland where they hoped to practise their religion more freely.

Preparations to leave England were accelerated by Brewster's appearance before the Court of the High Commission where he and three others were fined twenty pounds each for attending illegal services. After selling most of their possessions, the group made secret arrangements with an English sea-captain. As it was forbidden for anyone to leave the country without

The Separatists made unsuccessful
attempts to leave England

a permit, the captain had to be bribed. But the captain betrayed the group to the king's officers and they were imprisoned for a month.

The second attempt was in the spring of 1608. The women and children made their way by river barge to a lonely spot on the Humber estuary; the men walked the forty miles. Some of the men had been taken on board a Dutch ship when news came that armed men were approaching. So the ship sailed, leaving most of the passengers behind. They were arrested but not imprisoned for long because the authorities saw no point in it. The rest of the Scrooby Separatists managed to reach Holland in small groups at different times during the next few months.

Holland and new plans

One hundred Separatists, including members of the Scrooby group, arrived in Leyden in 1609 with John Robinson as their pastor, leaving Richard Clyfton and others in Amsterdam.

Though the men were mostly farming folk, they worked hard as weavers, carpenters and printers. They saved enough money to build their own houses; above all, they worshipped in their own way. In 1616 Edward Winslow of Droitwich, Worcestershire, arrived from London. With his help, Brewster set up a printing press which produced pamphlets denouncing the Church of England. These were smuggled into England and Scotland but were traced back to the press in Leyden. Brewster had to go into hiding to escape arrest.

Leyden

Although the Separatists enjoyed freedom of worship in Holland, they worried about the future and did not wish to lose their English identity. With Brewster now in hiding, they decided to seek permission from King James to emigrate to Virginia, in North America. This was eventually granted.

The New World was by no means unknown to the English. Elizabethan explorers had named a vast area Virginia in honour of the queen. Under James I trading companies were established to finance colonies. In May 1607 a colony settled at Jamestown, in Chesapeake Bay, but it was only due to the discipline imposed by John Smith that it survived. Captain Smith later explored North Virginia, renamed New England, and mapped the coastline from Maine to Cape Cod, whence he returned home laden with fish and furs.

A merchant, Thomas Weston, persuaded some of the Separatists to set up a colony in Virginia. His company of Merchant Adventurers would finance the voyage in return for five days' work a week for seven years. It was arranged that sixteen men, eleven women and nineteen children should sail from Holland on the *Speedwell*. Among the passengers were a few of the original Scrooby group: Mary Brewster and her two youngest children—the other three were to stay behind with the Robinsons in Leyden (William, still a hunted man, was to sneak on board at Southampton); the Carvers, the Bradfords and the Winslows.

Saints and Strangers

The danger and hardships to which all former emigrants to America had been exposed did not deter the Separatists. According to their own words, 'They were well weaned from the delicate milk of their mother country and inured to the difficulties of a strange land.'

Weston, realising that the success of the proposed colony depended on numbers, had engaged the *Mayflower*, a ship three times larger than the *Speedwell*, to transport about fifty-six people (cottagers, weavers, tanners and other craftsmen, small shopkeepers, servants and hired men) who were all seeking to better themselves. Such were John Alden, a cooper, and Priscilla Mullins, a shopkeeper's daughter, from Dorking, Surrey. In addition, there was a professional soldier, Miles Standish, to organise any military operations against pirates and Indians.

At last the supplies were loaded and the two ships sailed, the passengers full of misgivings. Ill luck dogged the *Speedwell*; both ships had to turn back to Plymouth where the Separatists transferred their baggage to the *Mayflower*.

Leaving Plymouth

On 6 September 1620 the *Mayflower*, Captain Christopher Jones at the helm, left Plymouth with one hundred and two passengers, their belongings, provisions, livestock (including poultry, pigs and goats), tools, firearms, lead for bullets, gunpowder and shot.

The Separatists were nicknamed 'Saints'—and were jeered at because they prayed so much. The other passengers were the 'Strangers', who were mostly members of the Church of England. Together they went as pilgrims to what they hoped would be their Promised Land. It was only later that they became known as the Pilgrim Fathers.

On board the *Mayflower*

Conditions aboard the *Mayflower* were cramped and there was little comfort or privacy. During storms the ship rolled from side to side, water dripping from ill-caulked seams. Food-stuffs which would not spoil were rationed: hard ships' biscuit, dried peas and beans, salt beef and pork, flour and grains. During the voyage weevils infested the provisions or mildew affected them. Beer was drunk as a protection against scurvy. The galley was tiny so little cooking was possible. Travel to America by sailing ship was to be hard for over 200 years. It was lucky that the *Mayflower* was a wine-trading ship and smelled sweet, unlike many ships which stank of rotting cargo.

Notable among the passengers were the Brewsters and the Bradfords from Scrooby, the Carvers and the Winslows.

After a voyage of sixty-seven days, land was sighted on the ninth day of November. In the grey morning light the Pilgrims rushed to the deck, some falling to their knees in prayer, others hugging friends and relatives in delight at their safe deliverance.

In spite of the length of the journey at the worst time of year, only one passenger died at sea: William Butten, servant to the Pilgrims' physician, Samuel Fuller. One child was born on board and appropriately named Oceanus; he was the son of Stephen Hopkins and his wife Elizabeth.

*On board
the* Mayflower

Landfall

The land sighted proved to be Cape Cod which was so named because of the swarms of fish found there in 1602. Captain Jones headed the ship for the Hudson River but was forced to put round again for the Bay of Cape Cod and to anchor there for the night. With winter coming on, he realised that it was much too dangerous to work a way along a virtually unknown coast. He felt that it was better to land where the ship was anchored and to stay there if possible.

There had been a great deal of friction between Saints and Strangers during the voyage. As Cape Cod was outside the area of the Pilgrims' contract, it was outside English law. It was vital for any colony that rules should be drawn up for the running of its affairs. So the *Mayflower Compact* was drawn up and signed by forty-two 'responsible men', declaring just and equal treatment for everyone. John Carver was chosen to be Governor for the first year.

Next day, a small boat set out for the shore with well-armed men on board to collect wood and explore. The land compared well with Holland and England; the soil appeared rich and fertile with a great variety of trees. The men returned to the *Mayflower* at nightfall, their boat laden with sweet-smelling juniper.

The Pilgrims went ashore on 13 November 1620, the women to wash the clothes while the men attempted to rebuild the boat which the Pilgrims brought from England, stored in sections on the *Mayflower*.

The first exploration

A party of sixteen men led by Captain Standish and including William Bradford, who was later to record the exploration, set off on 15 November on a two-day expedition. Each man carried a musket or sword and also a few provisions on his back.

They made their way along the seashore and soon caught sight of five or six people and a dog. At first they thought it was Captain Jones and some of his crew who had gone ashore previously but when the people ran into the woods, they realised that they were Indians. The *Mayflower* men marched for miles through valleys and forestland but there was no further sign of the Indians or where they lived. It was not until the second day that they found a spring of fresh water.

One of the main reasons for the exploration was to find the river sighted when the *Mayflower* sailed into the Bay of Cape Cod. During the search, Captain Standish's party came across a large tract of open ground that showed signs of cultivation and also mounds which had been raised as graves. Further

mounds, covered with sand, were found to contain baskets of freshly reaped Indian corn (maize). The Pilgrims took as much corn as they could carry. The river was finally discovered but there was no time to find out whether the water was fresh or salt. The party had to return: on the way they found an ingenious deer trap laid by Indians—it caught Bradford by the leg, much to the glee of his companions.

When at last they could see the *Mayflower* they fired their muskets and a boat was launched to fetch them. The explorers were met by Captain Jones and John Carver and given a hearty welcome.

Man armed with a musket and sword and wearing a breastplate

A site is found

While the explorers were away, the rest of the men gathered wood suitable for fuel and for rebuilding their boat; the women busied themselves on board the *Mayflower* washing and airing clothes and making their cramped quarters more comfortable. Another child was born, Peregrine, son of William White and his wife Susanna.

Because of the shallow water, the *Mayflower* was anchored three-quarters of a mile offshore. People who did go ashore at high-water times had to wade through icy water up to their thighs and most of them caught colds and coughs. To add to the discomfort they sampled mussels of an enormous size found on the beach and all of them, sailors as well as passengers, were terribly sick.

Another exploring party set off by boat to look for a suitable site on which to build a settlement. On 11 December, after

Exploring party at Plymouth

several days' search, the party landed at Plymouth, already named by Captain John Smith and marked on the chart of his voyage to New England in 1614. Plymouth had once been an Indian village and had large cultivated areas, now overgrown. There was a stream of fresh water and a steep hill nearby on which a fort could be built. The eighteen men, including William Bradford, Governor Carver and Captain Standish, surveyed the place, sounded the harbour and decided that Plymouth would make an ideal site.

The party arrived back at the *Mayflower* with the good news but were met by sad faces. Bradford was taken aside by his friend, William Brewster, and told that his wife Dorothy had fallen overboard and been drowned. Either she lost her balance as she stood on deck, or she was so sad at leaving her small son in Holland and so frightened of the future that she threw herself over the side of the ship.

The passengers were ferried ashore

Landing at Plymouth

The Pilgrims gave careful thought to what they heard about the Plymouth site and finally decided that it *was* the right place for them to settle. The *Mayflower* sailed as close to the spot as possible; on 20 December 1620 most of the Pilgrims were ferried ashore. It was icy cold when the men unloaded the ship's boats and the women carried ashore the first bundles of household goods.

Winter was upon them and it was vitally important to build a shelter against the worsening weather. They decided to build the settlement along the banks of the stream (to be called Town Brook) between the shore and Fort Hill where Captain Standish was soon mounting guard and drilling some of the men in case of attack by Indians.

On Christmas Day the settlers started to build the first rough huts.

The Separatists did not celebrate Christmas—religious holidays were against their beliefs. In any case, there was nothing to make merry with, as food and drink were in short supply.

The first homes

The first huts were probably made of wattles, branches and mud—the mud filling the gaps to stop draughts. A crude chimney was constructed of sticks and lined with clay, the roof thatched with grass or pine-boughs. Window-openings were covered with woven branches and twigs or oiled parchment.

These simple huts were common in England and quick to erect so they had to serve until the settlers had time to build more permanent timber houses. One of the first tasks was to fell trees in order to build a Common House that would serve as church and meeting-place for the entire settlement. It was built square, of rough-hewn planks, with a thatched roof.

The building programme taxed the Pilgrims' strength and they faced a bitter winter with the food stocks dwindling fast and the beer almost gone. Hunting produced a little game and fish for the common larder.

Nevertheless, the Separatists held their first formal service in the newly-built meeting-house on 21 January. All who were well enough came to offer thanks for the start they had made, but there were several who were too ill to attend.

*Building
the first homes*

'The Great Mortality'

Lack of nourishing food and the long journey had exposed the Pilgrims to anaemia, scurvy, pneumonia and other illnesses. People died nearly every day during January and February. By the end of February there remained only fifty of the original hundred or so Pilgrims. Of these fifty, only seven were well enough to tend the sick and to bury the dead.

In addition to nursing the sick in the Common House, there was the task of gathering the enormous quantity of wood for the fires which were needed for cooking, heating and boiling water to wash clothes and bedding. It was a wearing task, hazardous to their own health, but the seven, who included William Brewster and Captain Standish, undertook it willingly and without a grudge, thus saving the Pilgrims from a complete disaster during that first harsh winter.

Whole families were wiped out and only three, including the Brewsters, remained intact. Susanna White lost her husband William, Captain Standish his wife Rose and Edward Winslow, the printer from Droitwich, his wife. Indeed all but four of the wives died. Priscilla Mullins lost both her parents and her brother.

Orphaned children were adopted, widows cared for a widower's children, single men were attached to a fatherless family—everyone helped each other.

Nursing the sick

Indians

The Pilgrims spent the winter in fear of attack from wild beasts or men from the surrounding forest.

So, they were utterly amazed when, one spring-like morning in March, an Indian strode boldly into Plymouth. He astounded them further by speaking in their own language which he had learnt from English sailors fishing off the coast of Maine.

Samoset left next morning, promising to return. The following day he arrived with five other Indians carrying deerskins and beaver pelts. Beaver was then one of the most sought-after and expensive furs in England; the Pilgrims asked the Indians to find more.

A few days later Samoset returned, accompanied by another Indian who also, incredibly, spoke English. This Indian, Squanto, told them that he was a member of the Patuxet tribe which had lived at Plymouth. Squanto had been kidnapped and taken to Europe; by the time he got home his

Samoset strode in

tribe had been wiped out by a plague. So he had joined another tribe, the Wampanoag. This tribe, whose chief was called Massasoit, was the most powerful in the district.

Squanto was regarded by the Pilgrims as 'a special instrumente sent of God for their good beyond their expectation'. He was to excel himself as the Pilgrims' interpreter when Chief Massasoit and sixty of his men came to negotiate. A treaty was drawn up between Massasoit and Governor Carver. The Indians left, leaving Squanto behind to advise the Pilgrims.

The first harvest

After assisting the Pilgrims all through the winter, Captain Jones sailed the *Mayflower* back to England on 5 April, with empty holds. Remarkably, not one Pilgrim chose to leave his new home.

The seeds brought from England failed miserably, for the soil was unsuitable. Fortunately, Squanto had shown the Pilgrims how to plant Indian corn by placing four seeds in a mound of soil, with dead fish underneath to act as fertiliser. Squanto also taught the best way to trap deer and other game, where to catch the best fish, which plants and berries were safe to eat and how to make syrup from the sap of maple trees.

To the Pilgrims' great sorrow, John Carver, the first governor, died suddenly, probably from sun-stroke or a heart attack. William Bradford was chosen governor in his place. The same summer the first New England marriage ceremony took place between Edward Winslow and Susanna White, both of whom had lost their first spouses during the winter.

A special thanksgiving feast was held to celebrate the harvest in October 1621. (Thanksgiving is still kept as a holiday in the United States.) Enough wild turkeys, ducks and geese were shot to last for several days. Chief Massasoit and ninety braves attended, bringing five deer. The women baked plenty of corn bread to eat with the roasted meats, poultry and shellfish, and collected wild fruits and nuts to eat.

On the third day, Captain Standish organised an impressive military display for the entertainment of the guests.

*Squanto taught
the best way
to trap deer*

The arrival of the *Fortune*

The eleventh of November 1621 saw the arrival of the *Fortune*, bringing supplies and thirty-five more emigrants, including relatives such as Brewster's eldest son and Edward Winslow's brother.

The *Fortune* also carried across the ocean from England an important document legalising the Pilgrims' Plymouth colony which had so far been outside the area of North America covered by the Pilgrims' contract. It granted each settler one hundred acres of land after seven years of working for the colony.

Accompanying this document was an irate letter from Thomas Weston on behalf of the Merchant Adventurers demanding to know why the *Mayflower* had been sent back with her holds empty; unless the settlers made more effort to pay off their debt, no more essential supplies of gunpowder, shot, clothing, tools or foodstuffs would be forthcoming.

As the Pilgrims were already trading food, pots, tools and trinkets with the Indians for furs, and oaks and cedars could be felled and split into thick planks, the *Fortune* sailed back to England with enough beaver pelts and timber to pay off a large part of the debt to the Merchant Adventurers. As the ship entered the English Channel she was attacked by French pirates and the precious cargo stolen.

The Merchant Adventurers had paid for the *Mayflower*'s voyage and for the supplies that she carried; many things had still to be sent out from England if the new colony was to survive. So the Pilgrims' debt took many years to pay off.

Packing beaver pelts

Life in the settlement

Although Chief Massasoit was friendly, the colony was in fear of other Indian tribes. So work was started on fortifying the village with a stockade of palings eleven feet high. The stockade measured nearly a mile round and was not completed until the spring of 1622. A fort was later built on the hill where Captain Standish organised a constant watch.

Work on the settlement was from sun-up to sun-down; in winter, of course, livestock had to be fed by the light of a lantern. When the crops ripened they had to be gathered in before the fine weather broke, so every man, woman and child would help with the harvest.

At first, crops were grown on land which had already been cultivated, or on treeless ground by the seashore. Clearing land was one of the main problems. There were no oxen or horses

and tools brought from England were of poor quality. So the Pilgrims adopted the Indian custom of cutting a ring round the trunk of a tree, or peeling the bark, to stop the sap from rising; in time the tree would die and until it fell crops were grown beneath it. An axe was essential and every man was expected to use it ably.

Women worked hard, cooking foods strange to them with very few utensils, preparing and drying vegetables and fruits and salting down fish and meat. They also grew herbs and brewed special remedies against colds, fevers, fits, scurvy and many other ailments. The potions may not have cured but they gave the sufferer hope.

It became the custom that after the harvest many evenings were spent in communal corn-shuckings. A fire was lit in the Common House and everyone set to work. A blue or red ear of corn meant good luck for the finder.

Food and cooking

The Pilgrims had to adapt their English recipes to the new foods. They got some ideas from the Indians. Indian corn (also called maize) was used to make their familiar *hasty pudding*. Maize and beans cooked together in a pot made a dish called *succotash* to which fish was sometimes added. Maize was soaked to remove the husks and boiled until tender. This dish, called *hominy*, was sometimes eaten with butter and milk.

Various kinds of bread were made with maize-meal and cooked over the fire or in the ashes.

Hunting parties kept the colony supplied with game. There were also pigs, goats and farmyard poultry to provide meat. Fish was one of the main sources of food; it was often grilled Indian-fashion on planks of wood, picking up a smoked flavour as it cooked.

Vegetables were scarce, especially in winter. Each spring the settlers would look for young fiddle-headed ferns which gave relief from the monotonous winter diet of salt meat, dried beans, maize and maize-meal bread.

An iron pot might be the family's only cooking vessel. Meat and any available vegetable thrown into the pot to make what became *New England Boiled Dinner*.

All manner of fruits and berries which grew wild in the forest, were made into wines and cordials. Persimmons were found to make very good beer.

In order that the whole family could observe the Sabbath, beans were placed in a pot the night before to cook slowly by the fire and were served for all meals, with previously baked bread and cold meats.

A hunting party

Clothing

The Pilgrims wore clothing such as was worn in England at that time. It was certainly not enough to keep out the bitter winter cold in New England, Materials were usually of practical colours: greys, browns, russets and black.

The men wore jackets (or jerkins) and breeches. Even when made of leather they were torn by thorns and brambles and had to be constantly patched and mended. Deerskin was soaked in large wooden vessels filled with an oak-bark solution until it was pliable enough to be stitched up. Beneath their jackets men wore shirts of unbleached coarse cloth or finer linen according to their means. The shirts had large plain collars or, in the case of the wealthier Pilgrims, the ruffs fashionable in England.

Women wore bodices (or jackets) and skirts of wool serge or broadcloth, with a blouse similar to a man's shirt; also an apron of coarse linen or wool.

Underclothes were of the same fabrics, as were the night-shirts which were cut on the same pattern for both sexes. Children's clothes were similar to those of adults, little boys wearing little girls' dress until they were old enough to be 'breeched'.

Footwear varied from short hobnailed boots, called *start-uppes* to solid-looking shoes with rounded toes. Stockings were of coarse wool or made from cloth. People working in the fields often went barefoot. But footwear wore out—so *moccasins* were made of deerskin in the Indian style.

Men and women wore broad-brimmed felt or straw hats. Under their hats women tucked their hair inside linen coifs.

As hardly any clothes or fabrics arrived on the *Fortune* the Pilgrims soon looked a sad ragged lot.

Man wearing deerskin jacket and
breeches, linen shirt and woollen
stockings

Woman wearing woollen bodice and
skirt, linen blouse and coarse apron

Religion and education

Influenced by the teachings of Calvin, Knox and others, the Separatists had rejected the services of the Church of England. They read the Bible and had their own beliefs. They believed that the Sabbath should be spent in prayer. Only essential work, such as feeding livestock, was allowed.

Most of the other Pilgrims came to the Separatist services in the Common House. Men and women were in separate groups facing the preacher. They stood for the opening prayer which sometimes lasted an hour, and then sat for two hours while the sermon was given and a psalm sung—unaccompanied, as the use of any musical instrument was considered unsuitable.

In winter, people wore plenty of clothes in order to keep warm, sometimes resting their feet on hot stones wrapped in a bit of old cloth. In summer, the Common House was hot and stuffy and it was difficult to keep awake. An official, called a tithingman, poked people with a stick if they dozed off. He also kept his eye open for other unseemly behaviour. People who took part in games or idle talk on the Sabbath were reprimanded by the Elders, of whom William Brewster continued to be a respected leader until his death in 1643.

*A service in
the Common House*

He was a well-read man and
had brought books from England, mainly about religion.
Most families, Separatist or
not, owned a Bible which all
children were taught to read.
Writing was little practised,
though the Pilgrims' history
was recorded by William
Bradford—and later published
under the title of *Of Plymouth
Plantation*.

There was no school—everyone had to work. Some children, particularly orphans,
were apprenticed to a craftsman
or a household to learn a trade.
Sometimes, unfortunately, they
were treated as household
drudges.

Organisation and expansion

In 1623 two ships arrived with new settlers. Among them were Patience and Fear Brewster who had long been separated from their parents and three brothers. They found that each family had its own plot of land. The original idea was to run the colony on a communal basis, with work shared out according to each man's ability. But the Pilgrims found that each family would work harder on its own patch of land.

Obviously there had to be some kind of governing body to preserve order in the colony. Officials were elected annually by those who had a right to vote. As in England, this meant men who owned property. In practice, however, Separatist and non-Separatist had to prove to the community that he was God-fearing, hardworking and responsible. Unpropertied men and all women were excluded from voting.

In 1624 Edward Winslow, who had sailed back to England with furs and timber, returned bringing with him the first cattle that the Pilgrims had seen since they arrived.

At Duxbury

New England was not rich agricultural land. Expeditions were sent to trade with the Indians and to find new areas of land for cultivation. During one of these expeditions, in 1622, Squanto, without whose help the Pilgrims would have perished, died of a fever.

There was not enough room at Plymouth for all the settlers to make a good living. Several families decided to set up farms not far away. John Alden and Priscilla Mullins, who were married in the summer of 1622, eventually moved from Plymouth to Duxbury where they set up a home of their own—they had eleven children—and John lived there to be almost ninety.

The Promised Land

In spite of all the hardships of the early years at Plymouth, America proved to be the Promised Land for the Pilgrims.

They reported that herring, trout, oysters and lobsters could be dipped out of the water with a frying-pan! Cod was the most valuable fish, as it could be dried without losing flavour. There were deer in the surrounding country and many wild duck and geese. Partridges were said to be as big as English hens and the wild turkeys 'often killed in the woods (were) far greater than our English turkeys and exceeding fat, sweet and fleshy'. Berries, plums and nuts grew wild.

In all these things the Pilgrims were fortunate, for a bad corn harvest made living difficult and few supplies ever arrived from England. Commercial fishing was a failure.

The Plymouth colony was to be firmly established by 1628 and created a pattern of living for later and larger New England communities. Above all else, the Separatists were free from religious persecution and, although they did not behave tolerantly towards others, they could now worship God in their own manner.

Book list

The Pilgrims and Plymouth Colony, Feenie Ziner (Harper & Row)

Mayflower and the Pilgrim Fathers, Jackdaw No. 8, compiled by Richard Tames (Jackdaw Publications)

Early Stuarts 1603–1660, edited H. Boswell Taylor (Brockhampton Press)

The American Story in England, Eric Rayner (Shire Publications)

For the English background:

Illustrated English Social History, Vol. 2, G. M. Trevelyan (Pelican)

Women's Costume 1600–1750, Zillah Halls (H.M.S.O.)

Men's Costume 1580–1750, Zillah Halls (H.M.S.O.)

Index